PUFFIN

THE FAMI

John Yeoman and Quentin ~~collaboration~~ was on the school magazine at Sidcup Grammar School. They both went on to read English at Cambridge University, after which they continued to work together in what has proved to be an enduring creative partnership in children's books.

John Yeoman spent twenty-eight years teaching, for most of that time as Head of the English Department at the Lycée Français in London. He now devotes his time to writing stories and verse, as well as indulging his passion for gardening, the theatre, classical music and opera, and reading.

Quentin Blake began his career drawing cartoons for magazines such as the *Spectator* and *Punch*, but he is now best known for his distinctive children's book illustration, and as the creator of many best-selling titles. Head of the Illustration Department at the Royal College of Art from 1978 to 1986, he is now a visiting professor. In 1987 he was awarded the O. B. E.

John Yeoman

The Family Album

Quentin Blake

PUFFIN BOOKS

PUFFIN BOOKS

Published by the Penguin Group
Penguin Books Ltd, 27 Wrights Lane, London W8 5TZ, England
Penguin Books USA Inc., 375 Hudson Street, New York, New York 10014, USA
Penguin Books Australia Ltd, Ringwood, Victoria, Australia
Penguin Books Canada Ltd, 10 Alcorn Avenue, Toronto, Ontario, Canada M4V 3B2
Penguin Books (NZ) Ltd, 182–190 Wairau Road, Auckland 10, New Zealand

Penguin Books Ltd, Registered Offices: Harmondsworth, Middlesex, England

First published by Hamish Hamilton Ltd 1993
Published in Puffin Books 1995
1 3 5 7 9 10 8 6 4 2

Filmset in Baskerville

Made and printed in Great Britain by Clays Ltd, St Ives plc

We badger our parents, whenever we can,
To take us to visit our grandpa and gran.

And when we've all talked and had something to eat,
Our grandpa announces our favourite treat.
He goes to the bookcase (he's terribly slow)
And takes down a book from the very top row.
He beckons us over and, quick as can be,
We all snuggle down on the squashy settee.

While he turns the pages, our gran takes us through
The names and the stories, and tells us who's who.
THE FAMILY ALBUM: it makes us feel proud –
Our lot really are a remarkable crowd!

Belinda and Hattie

Belinda and Hattie, our elderly aunts,
Have crammed their whole house with extravagant plants.
They polish the leaves and they chat to each bloom
And they water the flower-pots that fill every room.

But just for a change, every once in a while,
They look at each other and give a sly smile,
And hitch up their dresses and fling off their capes,

And swing through the leaves like a couple of apes.

Cousin Ted

There's no one as sleepy as our Cousin Ted:
It takes all the neighbours to drag him from bed.

Whatever he goes to he's seven hours late;
At meals he ends up with his head in his plate.

Pizza was always his favourite

When visitors call they can tell he's indoors –
The caravan shudders to Cousin Ted's snores.

He once took a nap on a cold winter's day
And didn't wake up till the following May.

Cousin Charlie

Although Cousin Charlie is only just ten,
He's lived in the kitchen since goodness knows when.

His rich chocolate sponges, his golden fruit pies
And Viennese pastries have won every prize.
We peep through the window and thrill to the sight
Of marzipan slices, and strawberry delight,

And apricot crumble, and roast almond flakes,
And caramel custard, and cinnamon cakes,
And raspberry trifles, and fancy iced tarts,
And coconut fingers, and gingerbread hearts,
And no end of puddings, all served piping hot.

It seems such a shame that he eats the whole lot.

Annabelle-Jane

Our sister-in-law, who's called Annabelle-Jane,
Refuses to travel by bus or by train.
She says they're for cissies –

you see, what she likes
Are fire-breathing, customized,
super-powered bikes.

We clamber all over her latest machine:
>The chromium backrest's
>>a sight to be seen.
>The muddy exhaust-pipes
>>of fabulous size
>And waving antennae
>>cause gasps of surprise.

Done up in her helmet and goggles and chains,
She zooms up the highways and roars down the lanes;

She revs up the engine, and everyone quakes;

She weaves and she corners; she slams on her brakes.

And yet, when she comes back to our place to stay,
She sips at her tea in a lady-like way.

Uncle Ignatius and Auntie Diane

We call round to visit, whenever we can,
Our Uncle Ignatius and Auntie Diane.

They keep heaps of costumes inside an old chest;
We're always surprised at the way that they're dressed:

They're pirates,

or pixies,

or firemen,

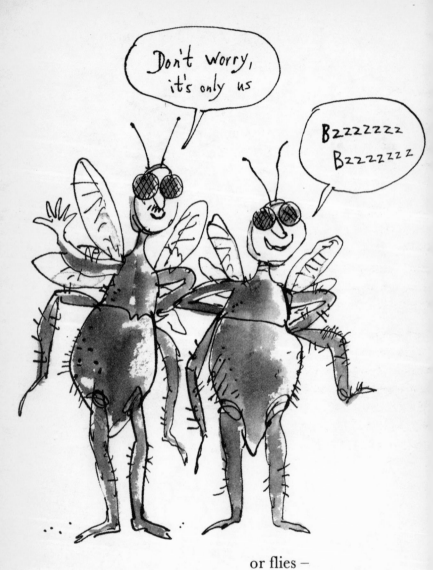

or flies –
They really have mastered the art of disguise.

Cousin Lucy

Our young Cousin Lucy is mad about paint;
Her most recent efforts have made people faint.
She painted her sheepdog bright blue for a lark,

And daubed orange stripes on the trees in the park.

And once when her mother was having a doze
She painted her green, with a deep purple nose.

And every so often she uses her skill
To make all the grown-ups believe that she's ill.
She does it by taking her brushes and pots
And covering herself in a mass of red spots.

Great-Uncle Bertie

Our Great-Uncle Bertie can give you a scare
By perching himself on the back of your chair.
He thinks he's a budgie, and wants to be fed
With almonds and pieces of dry toasted bread.

He nudges his mirror, he climbs up his cage;
His clothes are incredibly bright for his age.

He calls for attention by nibbling his door,
Or scattering his bird-seed all over the floor.

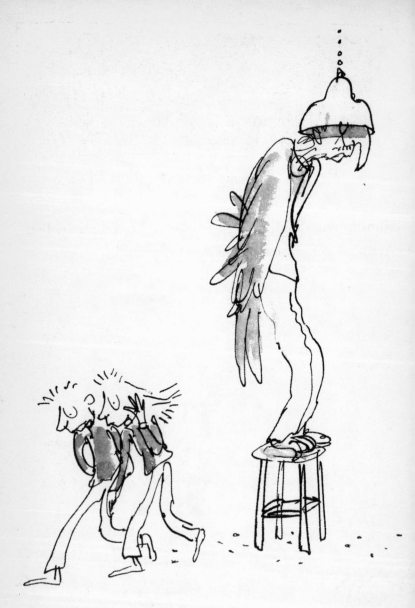

But when he gets bored with your stay, you can tell –
He shows you by sticking his head in his bell.

Aunt Lorna's Eight Daughters

Aunt Lorna's eight daughters, be-ribboned and frilled,
Are slim and athletic, and terribly skilled:

Secure on their trolley they juggle with bread;
The youngest piles seventeen cans on her head.

They scoop up bananas and cartons of cream,
This prize-winning Superstore Balancing Team.

They do a week's shopping in ten minutes flat –

Unless they bump into the manager's cat!

Uncle Marvello and Auntie Shazam

Our Uncle Marvello and Auntie Shazam
(To tell you the truth, they're just Eric and Pam)
Will always amaze you, whenever you go,
By giving their magical mystery show.

They take off their top hats and peel off their gloves
And, waving their wands, produce dozens of doves;
They conjure up flowers, and rabbits, and spoons,
And fill the whole room up with dancing balloons.

He makes someone's wallet and watch disappear,
And pulls out a long string of flags from your ear.
She smiles from her box with the swords sticking through,
And gives us a wave while he saws her in two.

And just when you're really enjoying the joke
They've suddenly gone in a puff of blue smoke.

Baby Cedric

Although Baby Cedric is too young to talk,
Or read, or play football, or whistle, or walk,
He doesn't just sit there. Oh, no, not at all:
He might not know much, but he knows how to crawl.

He scuttles up curtains; he skims across floors;
He's surely the speediest thing on all fours.

He won't be imprisoned in playpen or cot:
The top of the wardrobe's his favourite spot.

He's quiet as a kitten, and ten times as fast.
Thank goodness we always retrieve him at last!

Auntie Amanda

Our Auntie Amanda is light on her feet;
The people applaud when she twirls down the street.

She keeps a big trap which she sprinkles with rice
And catches no end of inquisitive mice.

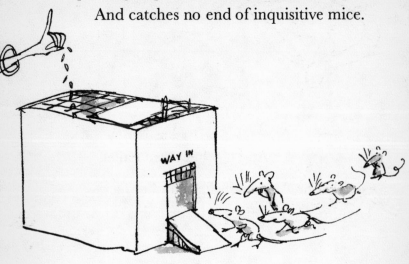

She takes them out gently by lifting the flap,

And teaches them ballet,

and Latin,

and tap.

Our relatives really are curious, you see,
So that's why we asked them all back home for tea.